KU-243-659

Praise for Brandon Sanderson:

'Anyone looking for a different and refreshing fantasy novel will be delighted by this exceptional tale'

Michael Moorcock on *Warbreaker*

'Highly recommended to anyone hungry for a good read'

Robin Hobb on *The Final Empire*

'Brandon Sanderson is the real thing – an exciting storyteller with a unique and powerful vision'

David Farland

'Sanderson will be forever mentioned as one of the finest fantasy writers of this generation'

Fantasy Faction

'Sanderson is clearly a master of large-scale stories, splendidly depicting worlds as well as strong female characters'

Booklist

MITOSIS

A Reckoners Story

BRANDON SANDERSON

GOLLANCZ
LONDON

The right of Brandon Sanderson to be identified as the author of this work
has been asserted by him in accordance with the
Copyright, Designs and Patents Act 1988.

First published in Great Britain in 2014 by Gollancz
An imprint of the Orion Publishing Group
Orion House, 5 Upper St Martin's Lane, London WC2H 9EA
An Hachette UK Company

A CIP catalogue record for this book is available
from the British Library

ISBN 978 1 473 20935 0

5 7 9 10 8 6 4

Typeset by GroupFMG within BookCloud

Printed in Great Britain by Clays Ltd, St Ives plc

The Orion Publishing Group's policy is to use papers that are natural,
renewable and recyclable products and made from wood grown in sustain-
able forests. The logging and manufacturing processes are expected to
conform to the environmental regulations of the country of origin.

www.brandonsanderson.com
www.orionbooks.co.uk
www.gollancz.co.uk

1

The day had finally arrived, a day I'd been awaiting for ten years. A glorious day, a momentous day, a day of import and distinction.

It was time to buy a hot dog.

Someone was in line when we arrived, but I didn't cut in front of her. She would have let me. I was one of the Reckoners – leaders of the rebellion, defenders of the city of Newcago, slayers of Steelheart himself. But standing in line was part of the experience, and I didn't want to skip a moment.

Newcago extended around me, a city of skyscrapers, underpasses, shops, and streets all frozen permanently in steel. Recently, Tia had started an initiative to paint some of those surfaces. Now that the city's perpetual gloom had been dispelled, it turned out all those reflective surfaces could make things *really* bright. With some work, instead of looking the same everywhere, the city would eventually become a patchwork of reds, oranges, greens, whites, and purples.

Abraham – my companion for this hot dog excursion – followed my gaze, then grimaced. 'It would be nice if, when we painted a wall, we would take a little more concern for colors that matched those of their neighbors.'

Tall and dark-skinned, Abraham spoke with a light French accent. As he talked, he scanned the people walking nearby, studying each one in his trademark relaxed yet discerning way. The butt of a handgun poked from his hip holster. We Reckoners weren't *technically* police. I wasn't sure what we were. But whatever it was, it involved weapons, and I had my rifle over my shoulder. Newcago was almost kind of peaceful, now that we'd dealt with the rioters, but you couldn't count on peace lasting long. Not with Epics out there.

'We have to use the paint we can find,' I said.

'It's garish.'

I shrugged. 'I like it. The colors are different. Not like the city was before Calamity, but also a big change from how it was under Steelheart. They make the city look like a big … chessboard. Um, one painted a lot of colors.'

'Or perhaps a quilt?' Abraham asked, sounding amused.

'Sure, I suppose. If you want to use a boring metaphor.'

A quilt. Why hadn't I thought of that?

The woman in front of us wandered off with her hot dog, and I stepped up to the stand – a small metal cart with a transformed steel umbrella permanently frozen open. The vendor, Sam, was an elderly, bearded man who wore a small red-and-white hat. He grinned at us. 'For you, half price,' he said, whipping up two hot dogs. Chicago style, of course.

'Half price?' Abraham said. 'Saving the world does not inspire the gratitude it once did.'

'A man has to make a living,' Sam said, slathering on the condiments. Like … a lot of them.

Yellow mustard, onions, chunked tomatoes, sweet pickle relish, peppers – whole, of course, and pickled – a dill pickle slice, and a pinch of celery salt. Just like I remembered. A true Chicago dog looks like someone fired a bazooka at a vegetable stand, then scraped the remnants off the wall and slathered it on a tube of meat.

I took mine greedily. Abraham was more skeptical.

'Ketchup?' Abraham asked.

The vendor's eyes opened wide.

'He's not from around here,' I said quickly. 'No ketchup, Abraham. Aren't you French? You people are supposed to have good taste in food.'

'French *Canadians* do have good taste in food,' Abraham said, inspecting the hot dog. 'But I am not convinced that this is actually food.'

'Just try it.' I bit into my dog.

Bliss.

For a moment, it was as if no time had passed. I was back with my father, before everything went bad. I could hear him laughing, could smell the city as it had been back then – rank at times, yes, but also *alive*. Full of people talking and laughing and yelling. Asphalt streets, hot in the summer as we walked together. People in hockey jerseys. The Blackhawks had just won the Cup.... It faded around me, and I was back in Newcago, a steel city. But that moment of tasting it all again ... sparks, that was wonderful. I looked up at Sam, and he grinned at me. We couldn't recapture it all. The world was a different place now.

But damn it, we *could* have proper hot dogs again.

I turned to look around the city. Nobody else had gotten in line, and people passed with eyes cast down. We were at First Union Square, a holy place where a certain bank had once stood. It was also the center of the new city's crossroads. It was a busy location, a prime spot for a hot dog vendor.

I set my jaw, then slapped some coins down on Sam's cart. 'Free hot dogs for the first ten who want them!' I shouted.

People looked at us, but nobody came over. When some of them saw me watching, they lowered their eyes and continued on.

Sam sighed, crossing his arms on top of his cart. 'Sorry, Steelslayer. They're too afraid.'

'Afraid of hot dogs?' I said.

'Afraid to get comfortable with freedom,' Sam said, watching a woman rush past and head into the understreets, where most people still lived. Even with sunlight up here now, and no Epics to torment them ... even with painted walls and colors ... they still hid below.

'They think the Epics will return,' Abraham said with a nod. 'They are waiting for the other shoe to drop, so to speak.'

'They'll change,' I said, stubbornly stuffing more of my hot dog into my mouth. I talked around the bite. 'They'll see.'

That was what this had all been about, right? Killing Steelheart? It had been to show that we *could* fight back. Everyone else would understand, eventually. They had to. The Reckoners couldn't fight every Epic in the country on our own.

I nodded to Sam. 'Thanks. For what you do.'

He nodded. It might seem silly, but Sam opening his hot dog stand was one of the most important events this city had seen in ten years. Some of us fought back with guns and assassinations. Others fought back with a little hot dog stand on the corner.

'We'll see,' Sam said, pushing away the coins I'd set down, all but two nickels to pay for our hot dogs. We'd gone back to using American money, though only the coins, and we valued them much higher. The city government backed them with food stores, at Tia's suggestion.

'Keep it all,' I said. 'Give free hot dogs to the first ten who come today. We'll change them, Sam. One bite at a time.'

He smiled, but pocketed the money. As Abraham and I walked off, Tia's voice, terse and distracted, came in over my earpiece. 'Do you two have a report?'

'The dogs are awesome,' I said.

'Dogs?' she said. 'Watchdogs? You've been checking on the city kennels?'

'Young David,' Abraham said around a mouthful, 'has been instructing me on the local cuisine. They *are* called "hot dogs" because they're only good for feeding to animals, yes?'

'You took him to that *hot dog* stand?' Tia asked. 'Weren't you two supposed to be doing greetings?'

'Philistines, both of you,' I said, cramming the rest of my hot dog into my mouth.

'We are on our way, Tia,' Abraham said.

Abraham and I hiked toward the city gates. The new city government had decided to section off the downtown, and had done so by creating barricades out of steel furniture to block some of the streets. It created a decent perimeter of control that helped us keep tabs on who was entering our city.

We passed people scuttling about on their business, heads down. Sam was right. Most of the population seemed to think the Epics were going to descend upon the city any moment, exacting retribution. In fact, after we'd overthrown Steelheart, a shocking number of people had *left* the city.

That was unfortunate, as we now had a provisional government in place. We had farmers to work the fields outside, and Edmund using his Epic abilities to provide free power for the whole place. We even had a large number of former members of Steelheart's Enforcement troops recruited to police the city.

Newcago was working as well now as it had under Steelheart. We'd tried to replicate his organization, only without that whole 'indiscriminate murder of innocents' thing. Life was good here. Better than anything else in the remnants of the Fractured States, for certain.

Still, people hid, waited for a disaster. 'They *will* see,' I muttered.

'Perhaps,' Abraham said, eyeing me.

'Just wait.'

He shrugged and chewed his last bit of hot dog. He grimaced. 'I do not think I can forgive you for that, David. It was terrible. Tastes should complement one another, not hold all-out war with one another.'

'You finished it.'

'I did not wish to be impolite.' He grimaced again. 'Truly awful.'

We walked in silence until we arrived at the first unbarricaded roadway. Here, members of Enforcement processed a line of people wanting to enter. People with Newcago passports – farmers or scavengers who worked outside of the downtown – went right through. Newcomers, however, were stopped and told to wait for orientation.

'Good crowd today,' I noted. Some forty or fifty people waited in the newcomer line. Abraham grunted. The two of us walked up to where a man in black Enforcement armor was explaining the city rules to a group in worn, dirty clothing. Most of these people would have spent the last years outside of civilization, dodging Epics, surviving as best they could in a land ruled by nested levels of tyrants, like Russian dolls with evil little faces painted on them.

Two families among the newcomers, I thought, noting the men and women with children. That encouraged me.

As several of the soldiers continued orientation, one of them – Roy – strolled over to me. Like the other soldiers, he wore black armor but no helmet. Enforcement members were intimidating enough without covering their faces.

'Hey,' Roy said. He was a lanky redhead I'd grown up with. I still hadn't figured out whether he bore a grudge for that time I'd shot him in the leg.

'How's this batch?' I asked softly.

'Better than yesterday,' Roy said with a grunt. 'Fewer opportunists, more genuine immigrants. You can tell the difference when you explain the jobs we need done.'

'The opportunists refuse the work?'

'No,' Roy said. 'They're just too excited, all smiles and eagerness. It's a sham. They plan to get put onto a work detail, then ditch it first chance to see what they can steal. We'll weed them out.'

'Be careful,' I said. 'Don't blacklist someone just because they're optimistic.'

Roy shrugged. Enforcement was on our side – we controlled the power that ran their weapons and armor – but they too seemed on edge. Steelheart had occasionally used them to fight lesser Epics. From what I'd heard, it hadn't gone well for the ordinary humans on either side of such a conflict.

These men knew firsthand what it was like to face down Epics. If a powerful one decided to step into Steelheart's place, the police force would be worth less than a bagful of snakes at a dance competition.

I gave Roy an encouraging slap on the shoulder. The officers finished their orientation, and I joined Abraham, who began introducing himself to the newcomers one at a time. We'd figured out that after Enforcement's cheerful welcome of stern gazes, strict rules, and suspicious glances, a little friendly chatting with someone more normal went a long way.

I welcomed one of the families, telling them how wonderful Newcago was and how glad I was they'd come. I didn't tell them specifically who I was, though I implied that I was a liaison between the city's people and the Reckoners. I had the speech down pat by now.

As we talked, I saw someone pass to the side.

That hair. That figure.

I turned immediately, stuttering the last words of my greeting. My heart thundered inside my chest. But it wasn't her.

Of course it wasn't her. *You're a fool, David Charleston*, I told myself, turning back to my duties. How long was I going to keep jumping every time I spotted someone who looked vaguely like Megan?

The answer seemed simple. I'd keep doing it until I found her.

This group took well to my introduction, relaxing visibly. A few even asked me questions.

Turned out that the family in my group had fled Newcago years before, deciding that the convenience wasn't worth the tyranny. Now they were willing to give it another go.

I told the group about a few jobs in particular I thought they should consider, then suggested they get mobiles as soon as possible. A lot of our city administration happened through those, and the fact that we had electricity to power them was a highlight of Newcago. I wanted people to stop thinking of themselves as refugees. They belonged to a community now.

Introductions done, I stepped back and let the people enter the city. They started forward, trepidatious, looking at the towering buildings ahead. It seemed Roy had been right. This group was more promising than ones who had come before. We *were* accomplishing something. And ...

I frowned.

'Did you talk to that one?' I asked Abraham, nodding to a man toward the rear of the departing group. He wore simple clothing, jeans and a faded T-shirt, and no socks with his sneakers.

Tattoos ringed his forearm, and he wore an earring in one ear. He was muscular, with distinctively knobbed features, and was perhaps in his late thirties. There was something about him....

'He didn't say much,' Abraham said. 'Do you know him?'

'No.' I narrowed my eyes. 'Wait here.'

I followed the group, pulling out my mobile and looking at it as I walked, feigning distraction. They continued on as we'd instructed them, making for the offices at First Union Square. Maybe I was jumping at nothing. I usually got a little paranoid when the Professor wasn't in town. He and Cody had supposedly gone out east to check in with another cell of the Reckoners. Babiar or someplace.

Prof been acting weird lately – at least, that was how we phrased it. 'Weird' was actually a euphemism for 'Prof is secretly an Epic, and he's trying hard not to go evil and kill us all, so sometimes he gets antisocial.'

I now knew three Epics. After a lifetime of hating them, of planning how to kill them, I knew *three*. I'd chatted with them, eaten meals with them, fought beside them. I was fond of them. Well, more than fond, in Megan's case.

I checked on the walking group, then glanced at my mobile again. Life was annoyingly complicated now. Back when Steelheart had been around, I had only needed to worry about – Wait.

I stopped, looking back up at the group I was following. *He* wasn't there. The man I'd been tailing.

Sparks! I pulled up against a steel wall, slapping my mobile into its place on the upper-left front of my jacket and unslinging my rifle. Where had the man gone?

Must have ducked into one of the side streets. I edged up to the one we'd just passed and peeked in. A shadow moved down it, away from me. I waited until it moved around the next corner, then followed at a dash. At the corner, I crouched and peeked in the direction the shadow had gone.

The man from before, in the jeans and wearing no socks, stood there looking back and forth.

Then there were *two* of him.

The twin figures pulled away, each heading in a different direction. They wore the same clothing, had the same gait, the same tattoos and jewelry. It was like two shadows that had overlapped had broken apart.

Oh, *sparks*. I pulled back around the corner, muted my mobile so the only sound it made would come through my earpiece, then held it up.

'Tia, Abraham,' I whispered. 'We have a *big* problem.'

2

'Ah,' Tia said in my ear, 'I've found it.'

I nodded. I was trailing one of the copies of the man. He'd already split twice more, sending clones in different directions. I didn't think he'd spotted me yet.

'Mitosis,' Tia said, reading from my notes. 'Originally named Lawrence Robert – an unusual Epic with, so far as has been identified, a unique power: he can split into an unknown number of copies of himself. You say here he was once a guitarist in an old rock band.'

'Yeah,' I said. 'He still has the same look.'

'Is that how you spotted him?' Abraham said in my ear.

'Maybe.' I wasn't certain. For the longest time, I'd been sure I could identify an Epic, even when they hadn't manifested any powers. There was something about the way they walked, the way they carried themselves.

That had been before I'd failed to spot not only

Megan, but Prof as well.

'You categorize him as a High Epic?' Tia asked.

'Yeah,' I said softly, watching a version of Mitosis idle on the street corner, inspecting the people who passed. 'I remember some of this. He's going to be tough to kill, guys. If even one of his clones survives, he survives.'

'The clones can split as well?' Abraham asked.

'They aren't really clones,' Tia said. I heard papers shuffling on her line as she looked through my notes. 'They're all versions of him, but there's no "prime" individual. David, are you sure about this information?'

'Most of my information is partially hearsay,' I admitted. 'I've tried to be certain where I can, but anything I write should be at least a little suspect.'

'Well, it says here that the clones are all connected. If one is killed, the others will know it. They have to recombine to gain one another's memories, though, so that's something. And what's this? The more copies he makes ...'

'The dumber they all get,' I finished, remembering now. 'When he's one individual, he's pretty smart, but each clone he adds brings down the IQ of all of them.'

'Sounds like a weakness,' Abraham said over the line.

'He also hates music,' I said. 'Just after becoming an Epic, he went around destroying the music departments of stores. He's known to immediately kill anyone he sees walking around wearing headphones or earbuds.'

'Another potential weakness?' Abraham said over the line.

'Yeah,' I said, 'but even if one of those works, we still have to get each and every copy. That's the big problem. Even if we manage to kill every Mitosis we can find, he's bound to have a few versions of himself scattered out there, in hiding.'

'Sparks,' Tia said. 'Like rats on a ship.'

'Yeah,' I said. 'Or glitter in soup.'

Tia and Abraham fell silent.

'Have you ever *tried* to get all of the glitter out of your soup?' I demanded. 'It's really, really hard.'

'Why would there be glitter in my soup in the first place?' Abraham asked.

'I don't know,' I said. 'Maybe the other boys dumped it in there. Does it matter? Look, Tia, is there anything else in the notes?'

'That's all you have,' Tia said. 'I'll contact the other lorists and see if anyone has anything more. David, continue observation. Abraham, make your way back to the government offices and quietly put them on lockdown. Get the mayor and her cabinet into the safe cells.'

16

'You going to call Prof?' I asked softly.

'I'll let him know,' she replied, 'but he's hours away, even if we send a copter for him. David. Don't do anything stupid.'

'When have I done anything stupid?' I demanded.

The other two grew silent again.

'Just try to curb your natural eagerness,' Tia said. 'At least until we have a plan.'

A plan. The Reckoners loved to plan. They'd spend months setting up the perfect trap for an Epic. It had worked just fine when they'd been a shadowy force of aggressors, striking, then fading away.

But that wasn't the case anymore. We had something we had to defend now.

'Tia,' I said, 'we might not have time for that. Mitosis is here today; we can't spend months deciding how to bring him down.'

'Jon isn't near,' Tia said. 'That means no jackets, no tensors, no harmsway.'

That was the truth. Prof's Epic powers were the source of those abilities, which had saved my life many times in the past. But if he got too far away, the powers stopped working for those he'd gifted them to.

'Maybe he won't attack,' Abraham said, puffing slightly as he spoke into the line. He was probably jogging as he made for the government building.

'He could just be scouting. Or perhaps he is not antagonistic. It is possible that an Epic merely wants a nice place to live and will not cause problems.'

'He's been using his powers,' I said. 'You know what that means.'

We all did, now. Prof and Megan had proven it. If Epics used their powers, it corrupted them. The only reason Prof and Edmund didn't go evil was because they didn't use their powers directly. Giving them away filtered the ability somehow, purified it. At least, that was what we thought.

'Well,' Abraham said, 'maybe –'

'Wait,' I said.

Down the way, Mitosis strode out onto the steel street, then reached back to take out a handgun he'd had tucked into the waistband of his jeans. Large-caliber magnum – far from the best of guns. It was a weapon for someone who had seen too many old movies about cops with big egos. It could still kill, of course. A magnum could do to a person's head what a street could do to a watermelon dropped from a helicopter. My breath caught.

'I'm here,' Mitosis shouted, 'for the one they call Steelslayer, the *child* who supposedly killed Steelheart. For every five minutes it takes him to reveal himself, I will execute a member of this population.'

3

'Well,' Abraham said over the line, 'guess that answers that.'

'His clones are saying it all over the city,' Tia said. 'The same words from all of them.' I cursed, ducking back into my alley, gripping my rifle tight and sweating.

Me. He'd come for *me*.

All my life, I'd been nobody. I didn't mind that. I'd worked hard, actually, to be precisely mediocre in all my classes. I'd joined the Reckoners in part because nobody knew who they were. I didn't want fame. I wanted revenge against the Epics. The more of them dead, the better. Sweat trickled down the sides of my face.

'One minute has passed!' Mitosis yelled. 'Where are you? I would see you with my own eyes, Steelslayer.'

'Damn,' Tia said in my ear. 'Don't panic, David. Music ... music ... There has to be a clue to his weakness here. What was his band again?'

'Weaponized Cupcake,' I said.

'Charming,' Tia said. 'Their music should be on the lore archive; we've got copies of most everything in the Library of Congress.'

'Two minutes!' Mitosis shouted. 'Your people run from me, Steelslayer, but I am like God himself. I am everywhere. Do not think I won't be able to find someone to kill.'

Images flashed in my mind. A busy bank lobby. Bones falling to the ground. A woman clutching a baby. I hadn't been able to do anything back then.

'This is what we get,' Abraham said, 'for coming out into the open. It is why Jon always wanted to remain hidden.'

'We can't stand for something if we only move in shadows, Abraham,' I said.

'Three minutes!' Mitosis shouted. 'I know you have this city under surveillance. I know you can hear me.'

'David ...' Tia said.

'It appears you are a coward!' Mitosis said. 'Perhaps if I shoot someone, you —'

I stepped out, lined up a shot, and delivered a bullet into Mitosis's forehead.

Tia sighed. 'I've got reports of at least thirty-seven distinct copies of him yelling in the city. What good does it do to kill one of them?'

'Yes,' Abraham said, 'and now he knows where you are.'

'I'm counting on it,' I said, dashing away. 'Tia?'

'Sparks,' she said. 'I'm pulling up camera feeds all over the city. David, they're all running for you. Dozens of them.'

'Good,' I said. 'As long as they're chasing me, they aren't shooting anyone else.'

'You can't fight them all, you slontze,' Tia said.

'Don't intend to,' I said, grunting as I turned a corner. 'You're going to work out his weakness and figure out how to beat him, Tia. I'm just going to distract him.'

'I've arrived,' Abraham said. 'They're already on alert at the government office. I'll get the mayor and council to safety. But if I might suggest, this is probably a good time to activate the emergency message system.'

'Yeah,' Tia said, 'on it.'

The mobiles of everyone in the city were connected, and Tia could dial them all up collectively to send instructions – in this case, an order to empty the streets and get indoors.

I dodged around another corner and came almost face to face with one of Mitosis's clones. We surprised each other. He got his gun out first and fired, a deafening crack, like he was shooting a sparking *cannon*.

He also missed me. He wasn't even close. Big handguns look impressive, and they have excellent knockdown force. Assuming you can hit your target.

I lined up my rifle sights, ignored his next shot, and squeezed the trigger. Just as I did, he thrashed, and a duplicate of him stepped away. It was like he was suddenly made of dough and the other self *pushed* out of his side.

It was nauseating. My shot took the first Mitosis, dropping him with a hole in the chest. He tried to duplicate again as he died, but the duplicate came out with a hole in its chest too, and fell forward, dying almost immediately.

The other clone, though, was also duplicating. I cursed, shooting it, but not before another version came out, and that one was already trying to clone itself *again*. I brought this one down just before it split.

I breathed in and out, my hands trembling as I lowered the rifle. Five corpses lay slumped on the ground. My rifle magazine held thirty rounds. I'd never considered that insufficient, but a minute of Mitosis cloning himself could run me out with ease.

'David?' Tia asked in my ear. 'You all right?' She'd have me on camera, using Steelheart's surveillance network.

'I'm all right,' I said, still shaking. 'I just haven't gotten used to people shooting at me.'

I took a few deep breaths, forced down my anxiety, and walked up to the Mitosis clones. They'd begun to melt.

I watched with disturbed fascination as the corpses decomposed, flesh turning to a pale tan goo. The bones melted after, and then the clothing. In seconds, each corpse was just a pile of colored gunk, and even that seemed to be evaporating.

Where did the mass for each of these new bodies come from? It seemed impossible. But then, Epics have this habit of treating physics like something that happens to *other* people, like acne and debt.

'David?' Tia said in my ear. 'Why are you still standing there? Sparks, boy! The others are coming.'

Right. Dozens of evil Epic clones. On a mission to kill me.

I took off in a random direction; where I was going didn't matter so much as staying ahead of the clones. 'Do you have that music yet?' I asked Tia.

'Working on it.'

I dashed up onto the bridge, crossing the river. That river would have made a great natural barrier for sectioning off the downtown, except for the fact that Steelheart had turned the thing into steel – effectively making it into an enormous highway, though one with a rippled surface. The river that had once flowed here had diverted to the Calumet River channel.

I reached the other side of the bridge and glanced over my shoulder. A scattering of figures in identical clothing had broken out of side streets and were running toward me, some pulling handguns from the small of their backs. They seemed to recognize me, and a few took shots.

I cursed, ducking to the side, heading past an old hotel with steel windows and a trio of flagpoles extending into the sky, flags frozen mid-flap. I almost passed it, then hesitated. One of the main doors had been frozen open.

I made a split-second decision and ran for that opening. I squeezed between door and doorway and entered the hotel lobby.

It wasn't as dark inside as I'd anticipated. I inched through a lobby with furniture like statues. Once-plush seats were now hard metal. A sofa had a depression in it where someone had been sitting when the transfersion took place.

The light came from a series of fist-size holes cut into the front windows, which were also steel now. Though empty, the lobby didn't seem dusty or derelict. I quickly realized what this was – one of the buildings that Steelheart's favored people had inhabited during the years of his rule.

I stepped on a bench by a window, leaning against it and peering through one of the holes. Outside, on the daylit street, the clones slowed in their chase, lowering weapons, looking about. It appeared that I'd managed to lose them.

'I would have the truth!' the clones suddenly shouted in unison. The effect was even eerier than seeing them all together. 'You did not kill Steelheart. You did not slay a god. What *really* happened?'

I didn't reply, of course.

'Your rumors are spreading,' Mitosis continued. 'People want to believe your fantasy. I will show them reality. Your head, David Charleston, and my empire in Newcago. I don't know how Steelheart truly fell, but he was weak. He needed men to administrate for him, to act as his army.'

The clones continued to stroll, spreading out. Several shook, splitting into multiples.

'I am my own army,' Mitosis said. 'And I shall reign.'

'You watching this?' I whispered.

'Yeah,' Tia said. 'I've got the city cameras, and I've dialed into the video feed from your earpiece. Shouldn't he be sounding dumber the more clones he makes?'

'I think something must be wrong in my notes,' I said. I'd been forced to burn many of my notebooks and keep only the most important ones. I'd lost many of my primary sources and speculations, and I could have easily gotten some details wrong.

Outside, Mitosis continued to duplicate himself. Twice, three times, a half dozen. Soon there were *hundreds* of him. They spaced themselves apart with careful steps, then, one by one, stopped in place. They closed their eyes, looking toward the sky.

What is he doing? I thought, clutching my rifle. I shifted on the bench, my foot scraping the wall. Outside, some of the clones nearest the hotel snapped their eyes open and turned toward me. Sparks! He'd created his own sensor network, using hundreds of copies of his own ears. It was clear to me now that the clones had more coordination to them than I had assumed. I slipped away from the wall, trying to step quietly. There might be a back way out of this building.

'Got it,' Tia said. 'Archive of pre-Calamity alternative metal albums in digital format.'

Her voice through the earpiece was incredibly soft. Still, outside, there was a sudden scrambling of footsteps. They'd heard.

They were coming.

I cursed and ran, leaping over a couch and scrambling toward the back hallways of the hotel.

There had to be a way out somewhere.

I passed through streams of light, holes cut like

spigots into the ceiling. The hotel had this flat building in the center and a tower to the side, many stories high. I didn't want to get trapped in the tower, so instead I turned down another hallway, passing a door that had been destroyed long ago. That light ahead was probably an exit for –

Shadows moved in through the exit. Clones, around a dozen of them, one after another. One pulled out a gun and leveled it at me, but when he squeezed the trigger, the entire thing shattered and turned to dust. The clone cursed, charging.

Huh? I thought.

There wasn't time for me to wonder. I threw myself to the side, entering another hallway. These were the administrative rooms of the hotel, behind the lobby.

'I'm trying to get you a map,' Tia said.

'No,' I said, sweating, 'the music.'

'Right.'

More clones that way. I was cornered.

I ducked into a room. It had once been some kind of clerical office, judging by the desk and frozen chairs, but someone had turned the desk into a bed with cushions, and there was even a wooden door affixed by new hinges attached to the steel ones on the doorway. Impressive.

I grabbed that door and slammed it closed. An arm got in the way at the last moment.

27

The clone grunted on the other side as I shoved, but other hands scraped around the doorway, grabbing for me. Each had an old wristwatch on them, and those snapped and broke as they rubbed on the door or wall. When the watches hit the ground, they shattered to dust.

'They're unstable,' Tia said – she was still watching via my video feed. 'The more clones he makes, the worse their molecular structure holds together.'

The clones forced the door open, throwing me backward. I whipped my rifle from my shoulder and got off one shot as a dozen of them fought into the room, heedless of the danger. Their clothing ripped easily, and when fragments fell off, they disintegrated immediately.

' "Albums by Weaponized Cupcake," ' Tia read.

The clones piled on top of me, hands gripping my throat, others pulling my gun away from me.

'Which one?' Tia asked. '*Appetite for Tuberculosis*? *The Blacker Album*? *Ride the Lightrail*?'

'Kind of getting murdered here, Tia!' I said, struggling to keep the hands from my neck.

There were too many. Hands pressed in closer, cutting off my air. Clones continued to clog the room, and those nearby began to split, making it difficult to move. They wanted to trap me in here.

Even if I got these fingers off my neck, I wouldn't be able to run.

Darkness grew at the edges of my vision, like a creeping mold. I struggled to pull the hands from my throat.

'David?' Tia's voice in my ear. 'David, you need to turn on your mobile speaker! I can't do anything. David, can you hear me? David!'

I closed my eyes. Then I let go of the hands holding my neck and forced my fingers through the press of arms. Choking, feeling as if my wind-pipe would collapse at any moment, I strained and got my fingers to my shoulder, where my mobile was attached. I flipped the switch on the side. Music blared into the cramped, suffocating room.

The clone directly on top of me started to shake and vibrate, like he was going to split – but instead, he began to melt, the flesh coming off the bones. The others nearby backed away in a hurry, smashing identical versions of themselves up against the walls.

I gasped in air. For a moment, all I could do was lie there, clone flesh and bones melting to goo around me.

Air. Air is really, *really* awesome.

The music continued unabated, a thrashing metal riff moving from chord to chord with the quality, almost, of a beating heart. The clones near me vibrated in time with it, their skin shaking like ripples in water, but they did not melt.

'So *awful*,' one of them said, a sneer on his lips. 'Jason couldn't write a riff to save his life. The same four chords, over and over and over.'

I frowned, then scrambled for my gun. I sat in the middle of the group of clones. Some had moved out of the room.

'That's odd,' Tia said.

I need a way out, I thought.

'Even the ones outside are vibrating a little bit, David. I can see it on the cameras. Surely they can't hear the music.'

'They're connected,' I said, coughing. I stumbled to my feet, holding my rifle in one hand, ripping the mobile from my shoulder with the other. I flashed it about, trying to ward the clones off. 'We need more music,' I said. 'A lot of it, loud as we can get it. That –'

The clones charged me. Ignoring the danger, they piled on top of me, reaching for my mobile, trying to rip it out of my fingers. Those nearest to me started to melt, but they still grabbed at my arm, fighting even as the flesh sloughed off their bones.

I backed into a corner, then noticed a sliver of light coming from above. A window, covered with a board.

To the sound of thumping rock music, I held the clones at bay, leaving a half dozen of them melting on the floor. Others gathered opposite me in the room, faces shadowed in the dim room. 'How did it really happen?' they asked in unison. 'Which Epic killed Steelheart, and how did you take the credit?'

'It's not like Steelheart was immortal,' I said.

'He was a god.'

'He was a cursed man,' I said, inching my way toward the window. The gooey remnants of bone and flesh steamed off me, evaporating, leaving my clothing as dry as if nothing had happened.

'Just like you are. I'm sorry.'

The clones stepped forward. I used the music to melt those who drew close, but they didn't seem to care. They marched on, falling to the ground, dissolving to nothing. They kept coming at me until only one stood in the doorway, though I could see shadows of a few more waiting outside. Why were they killing themselves?

One toward the back took out his handgun. It didn't break as he raised it. Sparks. Mitosis had just been trying to reduce his numbers to make the copies more stable.

I cried out, jumping onto the desk. I had to drop my rifle to rip the board off the window.

A large crack sounded from behind. I felt an

immediate thump in my right side, just under my arm – like someone had punched me.

Back in the factory, we would watch old movies every night, after work was done. They'd played on an old television hung from the cafeteria wall. Getting shot didn't feel like it looked in those shows. I didn't gasp and collapse to the ground. I didn't even realize I'd been shot at first. I thought the clones had thrown something at me.

No pain. Just heat on my side.

That was the blood.

I stared down at the wound. The bullet had ripped out a chunk of flesh just beneath my armpit before cutting through my upper arm. It was messy, all warm and wet. My hand didn't work right, wouldn't grip.

I'd been shot. Calamity ... I'd been *shot*.

For a terrifying moment, that was all I could think about. People died when they got shot. I started to shake; the room seemed to be trembling. I was going to die.

Another shot bounced off the wall beside my head.

You'll die way sooner if you don't move! a piece of me thought. *Now!*

I spun and threw my mobile at Mitosis. That worked; when the music got close, his clone wavered and melted. The mobile came to rest in the doorway, warding off those outside. I still had in my earpiece, though, which was connected wirelessly.

Somehow, I gathered the presence of mind to haul myself by one arm up and out the window. I tumbled into sunlight and collapsed to the ground outside.

I'd often heard that it wasn't the bullet wound that killed you – it was the shock. The horror of being hit, the panicked sense of terror, prevented you from getting out of danger and seeking help.

I slammed one hand over the hole in my side, which was worse than the hit in my arm, and squeezed the wound shut as I pressed my back against the wall.

'Tia?' I said. I figured I was still close enough to the mobile for the earpiece to work. I wasn't sure how far I'd have to go before I lost reception.

'David!' Her voice came into my ear. 'Sparks! Sit tight. Abraham is on his way.'

'Can't sit,' I said with a grunt, climbing to my feet. 'Clones are coming.'

'You've been shot!'

'In the side. Legs still work.' I stumbled away, toward the river. I remembered there being some inlets to the understreets there.

Tia cursed on the line, her voice starting to fuzz as I hobbled away from the hotel. Fortunately, it seemed that Mitosis hadn't anticipated my actually escaping this way. Otherwise, he'd already have clones back here.

'Calamity!' Tia said. 'David, he's multiplying. There are hundreds of him, running for you.'

'It's okay. I'm a rhinoceros astronaut.'

She was silent a moment. 'Oh, sparks. You're going delusional.'

'No, no. I mean, I'm surprising. I'll surprise him. What's the most surprising thing you can think of? Bet it's a rhinoceros astronaut.' The connection was fading. 'I can hold out, Tia. You just find the answer to this. Get some music playing across the city, maybe on some copters. Play it loud. You'll figure it out.'

'David —'

'I'll distract him, Tia,' I said. 'That's my job.' I hesitated. 'How am I doing?'

No reply. I was too far from the hotel.

Sparks. I was going to have to do this last part alone. I hobbled toward the river.

4

I tore off part of my shirt, wrapping it around my arm as I stumbled along; then I put my hand back to the side wound. I reached the stairs to the river and looked over my shoulder.

They came like a wave, a surge of identical figures scrambling along the street.

I cursed, then hobbled down the steps. Still, this was good. A terrible kind of good. So long as Mitosis was chasing me, he wasn't hurting anyone or trying to take over the city.

I reached the bottom of the staircase as the flood of figures arrived, some jumping over the sides of the rail to skip a few stairs, others scrambling down each step.

I pushed myself faster toward a set of holes drilled into the wall just above the river. Air vents for the understreets; they'd be big enough to crawl in, but not by much. I reached one just before the clones and clambered inside, kicking away a hand that tried to grab my ankle. I managed to spin around, facing the opening, and backed away into the darkness.

Figures crowded around the tunnel opening, cutting off my light. One of them squatted down, looking at me. 'Clever,' he said. 'Going where only one of me can reach you at a time. Unfortunately, it also leaves you cornered.'

I continued to back away. I was losing strength, and my blood made my hands slippery on the steel.

Mitosis crawled into the tunnel, prowling forward.

A lot of Epics liked to think of themselves as predators, the step beyond humans. The apex of evolution. Well, that was idiocy. The Epics weren't above humans. If anything, they were less civilized – more instinctual. A step backward.

That didn't mean I wasn't terrified to see that dark figure stalking me – to be confined in an endless tunnel with the thing as I slowly bled out.

'You'll tell me the truth,' Mitosis said, getting closer. 'I'll wring it from you, little human. I'll know how Steelheart *really* died.'

I met his gaze in the darkness.

'I wanna kiss you!' I shouted. 'Like the wind kisses the ra-i-ain!'

I belted out the song as loudly as I could. Tia had played it earlier, and I knew the words, though I'd been too distracted by the whole getting-strangled-then-getting-shot thing to listen closely.

I'd heard it as a child, played time and time again on the radio until I and pretty much everyone else got sick of it.

Mitosis melted in front of me. I stopped, breathing deeply, as a second clone crawled over the melting form of the first.

'Cute,' he growled. 'How long can you sing, little human? How are you feeling? I smell your blood. It —'

'I'm gonna miss you,' I shouted, 'like the sun misses the ra-i-ain!'

He melted.

'You realize,' the next one said, 'that now I'm going to have to kill everyone in the city. Can't risk them having heard these songs. I —'

Melt.

'Stop *doing* that!' the next one snapped. 'You —'

Melt.

I kept at it, though my singing grew softer and softer with each clone I killed. One of them found a knife and passed it up the line. That didn't melt; it just fell to the floor of the pipe each time one of them died. The next one picked it up and kept crawling.

Each clone got closer. I moved back farther in the tunnel until I felt a ledge behind me. The pipe turned down toward the understreets — and an assuredly fatal drop.

'I could shoot you, I suppose,' the next Mitosis said. 'Well, shoot you *again*. But then I wouldn't get the pleasure of cutting off pieces of you as you scream out the truth to me.'

I screamed out the next lyric, which proved to be a bad idea, because once I'd melted that Mitosis, I found myself slumping against the rounded wall of the small tunnel. I was close to blacking out.

The next Mitosis plucked the knife from the goo, holding it up and letting bits of his other self run down the blade and drip to the floor.

He shook his head. 'I was trained classically, you know,' he said.

I frowned. This was a change from the talk of torture, murder, and other sunny topics. 'What?'

'Trained classically,' Mitosis said. 'I was the only one in that band who knew his way around an instrument. I wrote song after song, and what did we play? Those stupid, *stupid* riffs. The same chords. Every *damn* song.'

Something about this tweaked a part of my brain, like a piece of popcorn on fire because it cooked too long. But I couldn't focus on it now; his talking had almost let him reach me. I sang. Weakly.

I didn't have a lot of energy left. How long had it been? How much blood had I lost?

This Mitosis wavered, but as my voice faltered, he came back.

'I am beyond you, little human,' Mitosis said, and I could hear the smirk in his voice. 'Now, let's get on with my questions.'

He reached me, took me by the arm, and yanked.

That *hurt*. Somehow, during all the running and scrambling, I'd never noticed the pain. Shock.

I'd been in shock.

Now that pain came crashing down on me, an entire detonated building of agony. I found my voice and screamed.

'How did Steelheart die?' Mitosis asked.

'He died at the hands of an Epic,' I said, groaning.

'I thought so. Who did it?'

'He did it himself,' I whispered. 'After I tricked him. He killed himself, but I caused it. He was brought down by a common man, Lawrence.'

'Lies!'

'Common people,' I whispered, 'will bring you all down.'

He yanked my arm again, delivering pain in a spike of agony. What did it matter what I said? He wasn't going to believe me. I closed my eyes and started to feel numb. It felt nice. Too nice.

Distantly, I heard music.

Singing?

A hundred voices. No, more. Singing in unison, the song that had blared earlier from my mobile.

Their singing was far from perfect, but there was a *force* to it.

'No. What are you doing? Stay back!' Mitosis roared.

All those voices, singing. I could barely make out the words, but I could hear the progression of chords. It actually sounded pretty, since I could ignore the awful lyrics.

'I am an army unto myself! Stay back! I am the new emperor of this city! You are *mine*!'

I forced my eyes open. Mitosis, in front of me, shook and vibrated, though the song was distant.

The clones were all connected – and if enough of them were hearing the song, the effect transferred even to the ones who weren't.

In a moment, the line of clones in the pipe screamed, holding their heads.

'Common people,' I whispered. 'Who have had enough.'

Mitosis exploded, each clone popping in a sudden burst. Their deaths opened up a passage to the light outside. I blinked against the abrupt sunshine, and despite the confines, I could see what was out there. People, standing on the frozen steel river, in a mass. Thousands of them, dressed in suits, work clothing, uniforms. They sang together, almost more of a chant.

The people of Newcago had come.

5

'You're unreasonably lucky, son,' Prof said, settling onto the stool beside my hospital bed. He was a solid man with greying hair, goggles tucked into the pocket of his shirt.

I flexed my hand. Prof's healing powers – gifted to me under the guise of a piece of technology – had mended my wounds. I didn't remember much about the last few hours. I'd lain in a daze, several city doctors working to keep me alive long enough for Prof to arrive.

I sat back against the headboard, breathing deeply, remembering the final moments with Mitosis.

They came to me clearly, though the time after that was muddy.

'How did she get them all there?' I asked. 'The people?'

'The Emergency Message System,' Prof said. 'Tia sent out a plea to everyone near the river, begging them to go to you and to sing along to the music she sent through their mobiles. They could easily have remained in hiding. Ordinary people have no business fighting Epics.'

'I'm an ordinary person.'

'Hardly. But it doesn't matter.'

'It *does*, Prof.' I looked at him. 'This will never work if they don't start fighting.'

'Last time the people fought,' Prof said, 'the Epics slaughtered millions and the country collapsed.'

'That's because we didn't know how to defeat them,' I said. 'Now we do.'

Prof sighed and stood up. 'I've been told not to antagonize you, to let you rest. We'll talk about this later. You did well against Mitosis. He ...' He hesitated.

'What?' I asked.

'Recently, Mitosis has been staying in Babylon Restored. Manhattan, as it used to be called.'

'That's where you just visited.'

Prof nodded. 'That he should come here when I went to scout Babiar ... it smacks of him coming intentionally while I was gone. That couldn't have happened, unless ...'

'What?'

Prof shook his head. 'We'll talk later. Rest now. I need to think. And son, as well as you did, I want you to do some thinking too. What you did was risky. You can't just keep rushing in, making snap decisions. You are *not* the leader of this team.'

'Yes sir.'

'We have an entire city's worth of people to worry about now,' he said, walking toward the door to the small room, which was warmed by sunlight through an open window. 'Sparks. That's the one thing I never wanted.' His face seemed shadowed in that moment. Grim, along with something else. Something ... darker.

'Prof,' I said, 'how do Epics get their weaknesses?'

'It's random,' he said immediately. 'Epics' weaknesses can be anything. They make about as much sense as the powers themselves – which is to say, none.' He frowned, looking at me. 'You know that better than anyone, son. You're the one who has studied them.'

'Yeah,' I said, looking out the window. 'Mitosis's weakness was his own music.'

'Coincidence.'

'Hell of a coincidence.'

'Well, maybe the weakness wasn't really the music,' Prof said. 'Maybe it was performance anxiety, or insecurity or the like. The music just reminded him of that.'

That was probably right. Still ...

'He loathed the music,' I said. 'His own art.

43

There's something here, Prof. Something we haven't noticed yet.'

'Perhaps.' Prof lingered in the doorway. 'Abraham sent me with a message.'

'Which is?' I vaguely remembered Abraham pulling me out of the tunnel and carrying me to the hospital.

Prof frowned. 'His exact words were "Tell him he was right about this city … so I'll forgive him about the hot dog. Just this once." '

Turn the page for exclusive Epic character sketches by Chris King

REGALIA

STATUS: High Epic

WEAKNESS: Unknown

THREAT LEVEL: ???

REGALIA

Before Calamity, Abigail Reed was an attorney, then a judge. Her
, however, was cut short, as she was offered her own television show.
show, *Judge Regalia*, brought massive ratings on daytime television for six years.
t to, as she put it, serve in a "better office." This turned out to be
t of Heaven Television Ministry, a televangelist program.
se of her passionate—but divisive—preaching, she soon became known as one
ca's most controversial religious figures. Shortly after Calamity, she gained her
rs on air. She then expressed a brutality and intolerance previously unseen,
enating most of her remaining followers.
ppened next is not fully understood. She destroyed her followers and moved
k City. She defeated the ruling Epic there and flooded
dubbing the city Babylon Restored.
here now.

GALIA, THE HYDROMANCER

al Name: Abigail Reed
ppearance: Distinguished, white-haired African American
woman in her 70s. Often wears a business suit.
urrent Location: Babylon Restored
onnections: Loyally served by the Epics Newton and
Obliteration

KNOWN POWERS

lass B Water Manipulation
Can control water en masse. Has used this power to flood
Manhattan, making the streets into rivers.

Class A Self-Projection
Can project an image of herself anywhere she wants, and
can see and interact through that image, but cannot be
hurt through it. As she uses this power constantly,
the location of her body is unknown.

Class C Divination
Can reportedly look into water to vaguely see the future.

KNOWN HIS

class Korean A

troubles began

school. By the e

Yumi was incar

to the prosecutor

case were murky.

With her newfound

the prison herself,

She settled in Ma

Newton's Third Law,

and Shade—she was

and earned her loyal

and terrorize the peo

NEWTON

Real Name: Yumi Park

Appearance: Teenaged girl—Asian. (Actual age is older.)
Dresses in retro-punk style and carries a sword.

Current Location: Babylon Restored

Connections: Serves under Regalia for unknown reasons.

KNOWN POWERS

Class A Force Redirection

Can redirect most forces applied to her back in the
direction they originated from. A bullet touching her, for
example, can be repelled with the same force, leaving
Newton herself unharmed.

Class D Enhanced Physical Abilities

Stronger and more dexterous than non-Epics. Has been
seen lifting a small car.

Class C Enhanced Speed

Has been clocked running at speeds over 60 mph.

born in the Queens Medical Center to upper-middle-
—one a lawyer, the other a publishing executive. Her
grade, when she was suspended for bringing a weapon to
ool, she had three convictions for dealing drugs.
ting trial for murder when Calamity arrived. According
d killed a rival drug dealer, though the details of the
as in juvenile detention when her powers manifested.
a prison break—or, well, she mostly just destroyed
s followed her out.
g the name Newton in reference to Isaac
he was a thorn in the side of such Epics as Meteor
-cracker they could not quell—until Regalia arrived
s Regalia's Fear Teams, who control the flooded city

STATUS: High Epic

WEAKNESS:
Nearsightedness,
Uncontrolled Teleportation

THREAT LEVEL:
Extremely Dangerous!

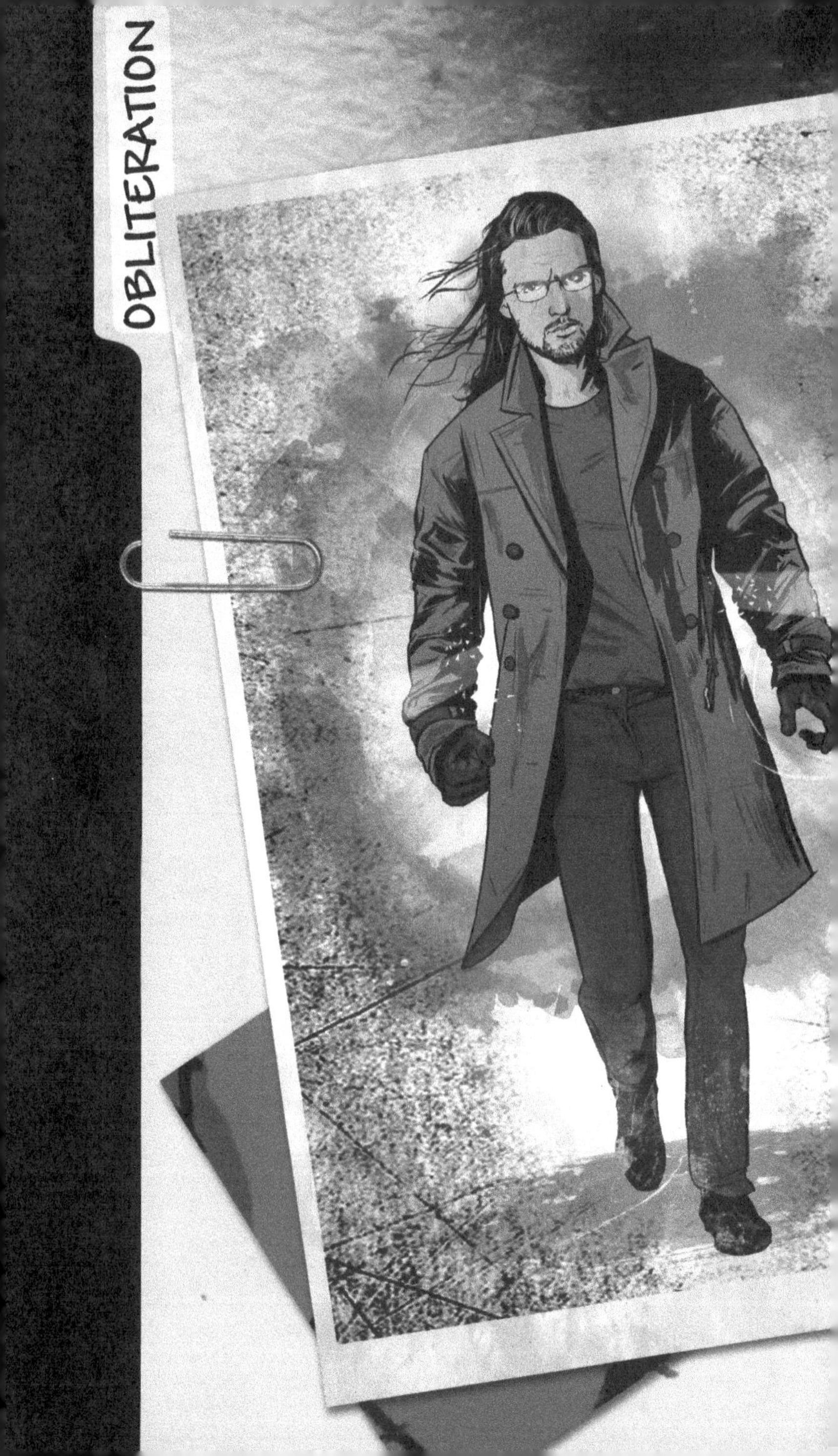
OBLITERATION

OBLITERATION

Real Name: Unknown

Appearance: Caucasian man in mid-30s with long dark hair, glasses, and a goatee. Usually wears a trench coat.

Current Location: Babylon Restored

Connections: Recently left Houston, where he was king, to join Regalia's court.

KNOWN POWERS

Class A Heat Manipulation

Can draw the heat from anything he touches, then expel it in an aura around him or into anything he touches.

Class C Teleportation

Can teleport to any place he can see, has been, or has had described to him. It does not appear that he can teleport anyone else.

Class D Danger Sense

Teleportation powers trigger automatically by instinct if he is in immediate danger.

HISTORY: Obliteration's history before becoming an Epic is completely _____. ___e first record of him is when he conquered Houston and became its tyrant. ___ since Calamity's arrival, he has become known as one of the most brutal _____ous Epics to ever live.

___rs can deliver such an intense burst of heat that they are able to _____ the invulnerability of even some High Epics. He heated Endless Dreams, a _____ invulnerable Epic, to a temperature said to match that of the sun, melting _____ and earning the fear of most who would oppose him.

___h his teleportation powers are limited, requiring a cooldown of a minute or two _____ uses, they make for a potent combination with his heat manipulation, allowing _____ appear suddenly beside opponents and destroy them.

___ntly, defying all logic, he left his throne in Houston and has joined with Regalia in _____ mer city of Manhattan.

Turn the page for a sneak preview of the sequel to Steelheart

Firefight

Prologue

I watched Calamity rise.

I was six years old then, and standing in the night on the balcony of our apartment. I can still remember how the old air conditioning rattled in the window next to me, covering the sound of Father's crying. The overworked machine hung out over a plummet of many stories, dripping water like perspiration from the forehead of a suicidal jumper. The machine was broken; it blew air but didn't make anything cold. My mother had frequently turned it off.

After her passing, my father left it on; he said that he felt cooler with it running.

I lowered my popsicle and squinted at that strange red light, which rose like a new star above the horizon. Only no star had ever been that bright or that *red*. Crimson. It looked like a bullet wound in the dome of heaven itself.

On that night, Calamity had blanketed the entire city in a strange warm glow. I stood there

– popsicle melting, sticky liquid dribbling down around my fingers – as I watched the entire ascent.

Then the screaming had started.

PART ONE

Chapter One

'David?' The voice came from my earpiece.

I shook myself out of my reverie. I'd been staring at Calamity again, but over twelve years had passed since Calamity's rise. I wasn't a kid at home with my father any longer; I wasn't even an orphan working the munitions factory in the understreets.

I was a Reckoner.

'Here,' I answered, shouldering my rifle and crossing the rooftop. It was night, and I swore I could see a red cast to everything from Calamity's light, though it had never again appeared as bright as it had that first time.

Downtown Newcago spread out before me, surfaces reflecting starlight. Everything was steel here. Like a cyborg from the future with the skin ripped off. Only, you know, not murderous. Or, well, alive at all.

Man, I thought. *I really do suck at metaphors.*

Steelheart was dead now, and we had reclaimed Newcago's upper streets – including many amenities the elite had once reserved for themselves. I could take a shower every day in my own bathroom. I almost didn't know what to do with such luxury. Other than, you know, not stink.

Newcago, at long last, was free.

It was my job to make sure it stayed that way.

'I don't see anything,' I whispered, kneeling beside the edge of the rooftop. I wore an earpiece that connected wirelessly to my mobile. A small camera on the earpiece allowed Tia to watch what I was seeing, and the earpiece was sensitive enough to pick up what I said, even when I spoke very softly.

'Keep watching,' Tia instructed over the line. 'Cody reports that Prof and the mark went your direction.'

'It's quiet here,' I whispered. 'Are you sure – ?'

The rooftop exploded just beside me. I yelped, rolling backward as the entire building shook, the blast spraying bits of broken metal across me. Calamity! Those shots packed a *punch*.

'Sparks!' Cody yelled over the line. 'She got around me, lad. Coming up on your north side –'

His voice was drowned out as another glowing pulse of energy shot up from the ground below and ripped the side off the rooftop near where I hid.

'Run!' Tia yelled.

Like I needed to be told. I got moving. To my right, a figure materialized out of light. Dressed in a black jumpsuit and sneakers, Sourcefield wore a full-face mask – like a ninja might wear – and a long black cape. Some Epics bought into the whole 'inhuman powers' thing more than others. Honestly, she looked ridiculous – even if she did glow faintly blue and crackle with energy spreading across her body.

If she touched something, she could transform into energy and travel through it. It wasn't true teleportation, but close enough – and the more conductive the substance, the further she could travel, so a city made of steel was kind of like paradise for her. It was surprising it had taken her so long to get here.

And if teleportation weren't enough, her electrical abilities also made her impervious to most weapons. The light shows she gave off were famous; I'd never seen her in person before, but I'd always wanted to see her work.

Just not from so close up.

'Scramble the plan!' Tia ordered. 'Prof? Jon! Report in! Abraham?'

I listened with only half an ear as a globe of crackling electricity whizzed by me. I skidded to a stop and dashed the other way as a second globe passed right through where I'd been standing. That one hit the rooftop, causing another explosion, making me stumble. Broken bits of metal pelted my back as I scrambled to the side of the building.

Then I jumped off.

I didn't fall far before hitting the balcony of a penthouse apartment. Heart pounding, I leaped in through the open balcony door. A plastic cooler waited by the door. I threw open the lid and fished inside, trying to remain calm.

Sourcefield had come to Newcago earlier in the week. She'd started killing immediately – random people, no purpose behind it. Just like Steelheart had done in his early days. Then she'd started calling out for the people to turn in the Reckoners, so she could bring us to justice.

A twisted brand of Epic justice. They killed whomever they wanted, but to strike back was an offense so great they could barely conceive it. Well, she'd see soon enough. So far, our plan to bring her down wasn't going terribly well, but we were the Reckoners. We prepared for the unexpected.

From the cooler, I pulled out a water balloon.

This, I thought, *had better work.*

Tia and I had debated Sourcefield's weakness for days. Every Epic had at least one, and often they were random. You had to research an Epic's history, the things they avoided, to try to figure out what substance or situation might negate their powers.

This balloon contained our best guess as to Sourcefield's weakness. I turned, hefting the balloon in one hand, rifle in the other, watching the doorway and waiting for her to come after me.

'David?' Tia asked over the earpiece.

'Yeah?' I whispered, anxious, balloon ready to throw.

'Why are you watching the balcony?'

Why was I ...

Oh, right. Sourcefield could travel through walls.

Feeling like an idiot, I jumped backward just as Sourcefield came down through the ceiling, electricity buzzing all around her. She hit the floor on one knee, hand out, a ball of electricity growing there, casting frantic shadows across the room.

Feeling nothing but a spike of adrenaline, I hurled the balloon. It hit Sourcefield right in the chest, and her energy blast fizzled into nothing. Red liquid from the balloon splashed on the walls and floor around her. Too thin to be blood, it was an old powdered fruit drink you mixed with water and sugar. I remembered it from childhood.

And it *was* her weakness.

Heart thumping, I unslung my rifle. Sourcefield stared at her dripping torso as if in shock, though the black mask she wore kept me from seeing her expression. Lines of electricity still worked across her body – like tiny glowing worms.

I leveled the rifle and pulled the trigger. The *crack* of gunfire indoors all but deafened me, but I delivered a bullet directly toward Sourcefield's face.

That bullet exploded as it passed through her energy field. Even though she was soaked with the Kool-Aid, her protections worked.

She looked at me, her electricity flaring to life – growing more violent, more dangerous, lighting the room like a calzone stuffed with dynamite.

Uh-oh …

Chapter Two

I scrambled into the hall as the doorway exploded behind me. The blast threw me face first into the wall, and I heard an audible *crunch*.

On one hand, I was relieved. The crunching sound meant that Prof was still alive – his Epic abilities granted me a protective field. On the other hand, an evil, angry killing machine was chasing me.

I pushed myself back from the wall and dashed down the metal hallway, which was lit only by my mobile, strapped to my arm. *Zip line,* I thought, frantic. *Which way? Right, I think.*

'I found Prof,' Abraham's voice said in my ear. 'He's encased in some kind of energy bubble. He looks frustrated.'

'Throw Kool-Aid on it,' I said, panting, dodging down a side hallway as electric blasts ripped apart the hallway behind me. Sparks. She was furious.

'I'm aborting the mission,' Tia said. 'Cody, swing down and pick up David.'

'Roger,' Cody said. A faint thumping sounded over his communication line – the sound of copter rotors.

'Tia, no!' I said, entering a room. I threw my rifle over my shoulder and grabbed a backpack full of water balloons.

'The plan is falling apart,' Tia said. 'Prof is supposed to be point, David, not you. Besides, you just proved that the balloons don't work.'

I pulled out a balloon and turned, then waited a heartbeat – until electricity forming on one of the walls announced Sourcefield. She appeared a second later, and I hurled my balloon at her. She cursed and jumped to the side, leaving red to splash along the wall.

I turned and ran, shoving my way through a door into a bedroom, making for the balcony. 'She's afraid of the Kool-Aid, Tia,' I said. 'My first balloon negated an energy blast. We have the weakness right.'

'She still stopped your bullet.'

True. I jumped out onto the balcony, looking up for the zip line.

It wasn't there.

Tia cursed in my ear. 'That's what you were running for? The zip line's two rooms over, you slontze.'

Sparks. In my defense, hallways and rooms all look very similar when everything's made of steel.

The thumping copter was near now; Cody had almost arrived. Gritting my teeth, I leaped up onto the rail, then threw myself toward the next balcony over. I caught it by its railing, my rifle swinging over one shoulder, backpack on the other, and hauled myself up.

'David ...' Tia said.

'Primary trap point is still functioning?' I asked, climbing over a few lawn chairs that had been frozen in steel. I reached the other side of the balcony and jumped up onto the railing. 'I'll take your silence as a yes,' I said, and leaped across.

I hit hard, slamming into the steel railing of the next balcony over. I grabbed one of the bars and looked down – I was dangling twelve stories in the air. I shoved down my anxiety and, with some effort, hauled myself up.

Behind me, Sourcefield peeked out onto the balcony I'd left. I had her scared. Which was good, but also bad. I needed her to be reckless for the next part of our plan. That meant provoking her, unfortunately.

I swung up onto the balcony, fished out a Kool-Aid balloon, and lobbed it in her direction. Then, without looking to see if the balloon hit, I jumped onto the railing and grabbed the zip line's handle, then kicked off.

The balcony exploded.

Fortunately, the zip line was affixed to the roof, not the balcony itself, and the rope remained firm. Bits of molten metal flew through the dark air around me as I dropped along the line, picking up speed. Turns out those things are a lot faster than they look. On either side, skyscrapers passed me in a blur. I felt like I was *really* falling.

I managed a shout – half panicked, half ecstatic – before everything lurched around me and I crashed into the ground, was rolling on the street.

'Whoa,' I said, pushing myself up. The city spun like a lopsided top. My shoulder hurt, and although I'd heard a crunch as I hit, it hadn't been loud. The protective field that Prof had granted me was running out. They could only take so much punishment before he had to renew them.

'David?' Tia said. 'Sparks. Sourcefield cut the zip line with one of her shots. That's why you fell at the end.'

'Balloon worked,' a new voice said over the line. Prof. He had a strong voice, rough but solid. 'I'm out. Had to take Abraham's mobile; mine broke in the fighting.'

'Jon,' Tia said to him, 'you weren't supposed to fight her.'

'It happened,' Prof snapped. 'David, you alive?'

'Kind of,' I said, stumbling to my feet and picking up the backpack. Red juice drink streamed from the

13

bottom. 'Not sure about my balloons, though. Looks like there might have been a few casualties.'

Prof grunted. 'Can you do this, David?'

'Yes,' I said firmly.

'Then run for the primary trap point.'

'Jon,' Tia said. 'If you're out –'

'Sourcefield ignored me,' Prof said. 'It's just like before, with Mitosis. They don't want to fight *me*, they want *you*. We have to bring her down before she gets to the team. You remember the path, David?'

'Of course,' I said, searching for my rifle.

It lay broken nearby, cracked in half in the middle of the forestock. Sparks. Looked like I'd messed up the trigger guard too. I wouldn't be firing it any time soon. I checked my thigh holster and the handgun there. It seemed good. Well, as good as a handgun can be. I hate the things.

'Flashes in the windows of that apartment complex, moving down,' Cody said from the copter. 'She's teleporting along the outer wall, heading toward the ground. Chasing you, David.'

'I don't like this,' Tia noted. 'I think we should abort.'

'David thinks he can do this,' Prof said. 'And I trust him.'

Despite the danger of the moment, I smiled. I hadn't realized until joining the Reckoners just how lonely my life had been. Now, to hear words like those …

Well, it felt good. Really good.

'I'm bait,' I said over the line, positioning myself to wait for Sourcefield and searching in my back-pack for unbroken balloons. I had two left. 'Tia, get our troops into position.'

'Roger,' she said reluctantly.

I moved down the street. Lanterns hung from the old, useless street lamps nearby, giving me light. By it, I caught sight of some faces peeking through windows. The windows had no glass, just old-fash-ioned wooden shutters we'd cut and placed there.

In assassinating Steelheart, the Reckoners had basically declared all-out war on the Epics. Some people had fled Newcago, fearing retribution – but most people had stayed here, and others had come. During the months since Steelheart's fall, we'd almost doubled the population of Newcago.

I nodded to those people watching. I wouldn't shoo them back to safety. We, the Reckoners, were their champions – but someday, these people would have to stand on their own against the Epics. I wanted them to watch.

'Cody, do you have a visual?' I asked into my mobile.

'No,' Cody said. 'She should be coming any moment …' The dark shadow of his copter passed overhead. Enforcement — Steelheart's police force — was ours now. I wasn't sure what I thought of that. Enforcement had done its best to kill me on several occasions. You didn't just 'get over' something like that.

In fact, they *had* killed Megan. She'd recovered. Mostly. I felt at the gun in my holster. It had been one of hers.

'I'm getting into position with troops,' Abraham said.

'David? Any sign of Sourcefield?' Tia asked.

'No,' I said, looking down the deserted street. Empty of people, lit by a few lonely lanterns, the city almost felt like it had back in Steelheart's days. Desolate and dark. Where was Sourcefield?

She can teleport through walls, I thought. *What would I do in her case, if I could do the same?* We had the tensors, which let us tunnel through basically anything we wanted. Close enough. What would I do if I had those now?

The answer to that was obvious. I'd go down.

She was underneath me.

Chapter Three

'She's gone into the understreets!' I said, pulling out one of my two remaining water balloons. 'She's going to come up nearby, try to surprise me.'

Even as I said it, lightning moved across the street, and a glowing figure materialized up through the ground.

I hurled my Kool-Aid balloon, then ran.

I heard it splat, then heard Sourcefield curse. Since no energy blasts tried to fry me, I assumed that I'd hit.

'I'm going to destroy you, little man!' Sourcefield yelled after me. 'I'll rip you apart like a piece of tissue paper in a hurricane!'

'Wow,' I said, reaching an intersection and taking cover by an old mailbox.

'What?' Tia asked.

'That was a good metaphor.'

I glanced back at Sourcefield. She strode down the street, alight with electricity. Lines of it flew from her to the street, to nearby poles, and to the walls of the buildings. Such *power*. Was this what Edmund – the kindly Epic who powered Newcago for us – would be like, if he weren't constantly gifting his abilities away?

'I refuse to believe,' the woman shouted, 'that you killed Steelheart!'

Mitosis said the same thing, I thought. He'd been another Epic who had come to Newcago recently. They couldn't accept that one of their most powerful – an Epic that even others like Sourcefield had feared – had been killed by common men.

She looked grand, all in black with the fluttering cape, electricity leaping from her in sparks and flashes. Unfortunately, I didn't need her grand. I needed her *angry*. Some members of Enforcement crept out of a building nearby, carrying assault rifles on their backs and Kool-Aid balloons in their hands. I motioned them toward an alley. They nodded and pulled back to wait.

It was time for me to taunt an Epic.

'I didn't kill only Steelheart!' I shouted at her. 'I've killed dozens of Epics. I'll kill you too!'

An energy blast hit my mailbox. I dove for cover behind a building, and another blast hit the ground only inches from where I crouched. As I brushed the ground with my arm, a *shock* ran up it, jolting me. I cursed, putting my back to the wall and shaking away the pain in my hand, then peeked around the side of the building. Sourcefield was running at me.

Great! Also, *terrifying*.

I dashed for a doorway across the street. Sourcefield tore around the corner just as I entered the building.

Inside, a path had been cleared through what had once been some kind of car showroom. I ran straight through it, and Sourcefield followed, teleporting though the front wall at speed.

I dashed through room after room, following the pattern we'd set out earlier.

Right, duck through that room.

Left down a hallway.

Right again.

We'd used another of Prof's powers – the one he disguised as technology called the tensors – to drill doorways. Sourcefield followed on my tail, passing through walls in flashes of light. I never stayed in her sight long enough for her to get off a good shot. This was perfect. She ...

... she slowed down.

I stopped beside the door out the back of the building. Sourcefield had stopped following. She stood at the end of a long hallway leading to my door, electricity zipping from her to the steel walls.

'Tia, you see this?' I whispered.

'Yeah. Looks like something spooked her.'

I took a deep breath. It was far less than ideal, but ... 'Abraham,' I whispered, 'bring the troops in. Full-out attack.'

'Agreed,' Prof said.

The enforcement troops who had been lying in wait stormed in through the front of the car dealership building. Others came down the steps from above; I heard their tromping footfalls. Sourcefield glanced back as a pair of soldiers entered the hallway in full gear, with helms and futuristic armor. That they were lobbing bright orange water balloons slightly spoiled the coolness of the effect.

Sourcefield laid a hand on the wall beside her, then transformed into electricity and melded into the steel, disappearing. The balloons broke uselessly on the floor of the corridor.

Sourcefield emerged back into the hallway and released bursts of energy down the corridor. I squeezed my eyes shut as the shots blasted the two soldiers, but I couldn't block out their cries.

'This the best the infamous Reckoners can do?' Sourcefield shouted as more soldiers came in, throwing water balloons from all directions. I forced myself to watch, pulling out my handgun, as Sourcefield dropped through the floor.

She came up behind a group of soldiers in the middle of the corridor. The men screamed as the electricity took them. I gritted my teeth. If they lived, Prof would be able to heal them under the guise of using 'Reckoner technology.'

'The balloons aren't working,' Tia said.

'They are,' I hissed, watching as one hit Sourcefield. Her powers wavered. I took a shot, as did three Enforcement gunmen who had set up opposite me at the far end of the corridor.

All four bullets hit; all four were caught in her energy field and destroyed. The balloons were working, just not well enough.

'All units on the southern side of the corridor,' Abraham's voice said, 'pull back. Immediately.'

I ducked out the door as a sudden barrage of bullets shook the building. Abraham, who had set up behind the Enforcement sharpshooters at the far end of the corridor, was unloading with his XM380 gravatonic minigun.

I grabbed my mobile and patched into Abraham's video feed. I could see it from his perspective, gun flashing in the dark, bullet after bullet ricocheting down the steel corridor, throwing sparks. Any that reached Sourcefield *still* got trapped or deflected by her electric field. A group of men and women behind Abraham threw balloon after balloon. Above, soldiers pulled back a trapdoor in the ceiling and prepared to dump a bucket of Kool-Aid.

Sourcefield jumped away, dodging the poured bucket. Step by step, she retreated from that splashing liquid. She *was* afraid of the stuff, but it wasn't working completely. An Epic's weakness was supposed to negate their powers totally, and this wasn't doing so.

I was pretty sure I knew why.

Sourcefield unleashed a barrage of energy blasts toward Abraham and the others. Abraham cursed and went down, but his protective field – gifted to him by Prof under the guise of a jacket with a technological forcefield – shielded him and sheltered the people behind him. I heard groans through the feed, though I couldn't see anything. I turned off the feed.

'You are *nothing*!' Sourcefield shouted.

I strapped the mobile back to my arm and stepped back into the hallway in time to see her sending a wave of electricity up through the ceiling toward those above. Screams.

I hefted my last water balloon, then threw it. It exploded across her back.

Sourcefield spun on me. Sparks! A High Epic in her glory, energy flaring … Was it any wonder that these things presumed to rule?

I spat at her feet, then turned and ran out the back door.

She shouted angrily, and followed after me.

'Upper units, Haven Street,' Tia said in my ear, 'get ready to lob.'

People appeared on the top of the building I'd just left, and they hurled water balloons down as Sourcefield broke out after me. She ignored them, following me. If anything, the falling balloons just made her more mad.

When they splashed near her, however, she stopped shouting.

Right, I thought, sweating, slamming my way into the building across the street. It was a small apartment complex. I ran through the entryway and into the first apartment.

Sourcefield followed in a storm of energy and anger. She didn't stop for walls; she passed through them in flashes of light.

Just a little further! I urged silently as I shut a door. This complex was populated, and we'd replaced many of the frozen steel doors with wooden ones that worked.

Sourcefield came through the wall as I leaped over a steel couch and entered the next room — which was pitch black inside. I slammed the door.

The light of Sourcefield entering blinded me. Her aura hit, and that little shock I'd taken earlier suddenly seemed miniscule. Electricity shot through me, causing my muscles to go weak and spasm. I reached to press the large button on the wall, but my arms weren't working right.

I slammed my face into it instead.

I collapsed, succumbing to the shock of her energy. Above, the ceiling of the small, darkened room – which had once been a bathroom – opened up, dumping several hundred gallons of Kool-Aid down on us. Above that, showerheads turned on, spraying more of the red liquid.

Sourcefield's energy dampened dramatically. Electricity ran up her arms in little ribbons, but kept shorting out. She reached for the door, but it had locked after me. Cursing, she held up a fist, trying to summon the energy to teleport, but the constant rain of liquid disrupted her powers.

I struggled to my knees.

She turned on me and growled, then seized me by the shoulders.

I reached up, grabbing her mask by the front, then yanking it off. It had a plastic piece on the front that obviously fit over the nose and mouth. A filter of some sort?

Beneath the mask, she was a middle-aged woman with curly brown hair. The liquid continued to rain down, and ran in streams along her cheeks, across her lips. Getting into her mouth.

Her light went out completely.

I groaned, climbing to my feet as Sourcefield shouted in panic, scrambling at the door, rattling it, trying to get it to open. I tapped my mobile, bathing the room in a soft white light.

'I'm sorry,' I said, raising Megan's handgun to the Epic's head.

Sourcefield looked to me, eyes widening.

I squeezed the trigger. This time, the bullet didn't bounce off. She fell to the ground, and a deeper red liquid began to pool around her, mixing with what was raining down. I lowered the gun.

My name is David Charleston.

I kill people with super powers.